Hooked by the BBC 2

Exploring Boundaries,
Facing Truths

Book 2 in the *Hooked by the BBC Series*

Amber Carden

CHAPTER ONE: The Conversation 1

CHAPTER TWO: The Invitation 12

CHAPTER THREE: The Next Step 26

CHAPTER FOUR: Dangerous Dealings 40

CHAPTER FIVE: The Confrontation 54

CHAPTER SIX: The Proposal 66

CHAPTER ONE: The Conversation

It had been a couple of days since Sam had kicked Jay out of her house. Since then, she had woken up everyday to calls, texts and emails from him asking for her to talk to him. She didn't want to entertain him anymore because she had the feeling that it was only going to be a matter of time before he overstepped boundaries again but she had to admit to herself that it was incredibly tempting.

Jay was a big part of her sexual awakening and it was hard to let someone who had been an integral part of that go. Sending him away was the right choice, she knew this but did this mean that she would have to go back to mundane sex with her husband?

She loved Mike, her heart would always belong to him but how could she go back to finishing herself off in the bathroom every time they had her after she had experienced some of the most intense orgasms of her life in the hands of Jay. When her thoughts went that way, it made her contemplate taking up her phone and reaching out to him again, this time with stronger boundaries.

But she knew that would be futile, what if a situation came where she was high on oxytocin and he manipulated her into leaving her husband for him. That was not a scenario that she wanted to entertain in the slightest.

It would only be a matter of time before he became possessive and that was energy that she wouldn't want in her marriage, not when Mike had been so understanding of her wants and needs.

After the last time they met, Mike had watched the video and had of course, found it very arousing. He had asked her when she and Jay would be meeting up again so he could be a part of their tryst this time but she had hesitated to answer him. When he pressed her, she had no choice but to come clean.

"I don't think we'll be seeing Jay anymore." She had said cryptically.

Mike had raised an eyebrow, curious. "Did something happen with you two? Oh my goodness did he disrespect you in some way? I'll kill him if he upset you." Mike had said, getting all protective.

Sam laughed. Mike was well into his 40s with back pain that made him take painkillers periodically. If he tries to go up against Jay, he would end up in the hospital. Still though, she appreciated his concern and liked that he was still willing to fight for her honor like they were kids again.

"No, he didn't do anything to me. Well, he didn't do anything that I didn't like anyway." Sam said, smiling to herself.

"So what's the problem?" Mike asked, raising his eyebrow once again.

"I'm just bored." Sam said, lying through her teeth. She didn't want to tell Mike the real reason that she had cut things off with Jay, she didn't want to get into it but she still had to give him something so he would get off her back.

"Bored? You've only been with him a couple of times, how could you be bored already?" Mike pressed.

"People can get bored Mike. It happens all the time, maybe I'm ready for something new, I don't know. I just know that I don't want to get involved with Jay anymore, can't you respect that?" Sam said, feigning anger. Maybe if she acted like she was upset, Mike would drop it.

Like she anticipated, Mike dropped the matter and didn't bring it up anymore after the day. That left Sam enough time to process everything that happened on her own time.

At the end of the day, she had realized that Jay's attitude was a red flag but that didn't mean that she didn't want to continue exploring this new side of herself. She hoped that Mike would be understanding when she told him everything that happened.

The next weekend that followed the day Sam kicked Jay out of her house, she got up early as she had spent the night before scrolling online forums for people who were perhaps in a similar situation as hers. People who wanted to enjoy other men, preferably BBCs but still wanted to preserve the relationships with her partners. She hadn't found much but that didn't deter her from wanting to keep searching.

She was making herself some coffee, contemplating everything that had happened when she heard the sound of footsteps. No doubt they were Mike's but they still made her tense.

He walked into the kitchen in a robe, rubbing his eyes as he made his way towards her. She smiled to herself, he was kind of cute even after all this time.

"Morning," Mike said to his wife as he walked into the kitchen. He grabbed a mug from the counter and poured himself some coffee. "You're up early."

Sam was leaning against the kitchen counter nursing a mug of coffee of her own. She had been thinking about the incident from the days before when she sent Jay out of her house after having incredible sex with him. It was great but she had an inkling that if she continued, her relationship with her husband would be undermined and that was something she did not want to deal with.

"Yeah, I couldn't sleep. I've been thinking about...stuff." She said cryptically.

Mike took a sip out of the mug in his hands then leaned against the counter beside her. "Let me guess, this is about Jay? You know, you never really told me what happened between you two. Based on the video I watched from the last time you hooked up with him, everything looked great."

"It was great still he basically told me that it was only a matter of time till I left you for him."

"He said that?" Mike asked, his brow furrowed.

"Yeah he did and I told him that wasn't going to be the case. It was just out of nowhere because when we started all this I thought we made it clear where we stood on the whole thing. The intention was to have a little fun, to explore and I thought he understood that."

Mike looked deep in thought, trying to process everything Sam had just said. He was a little conflicted; on the one hand he was happy that his wife stood up for them but on the other he was confused because what if she was denying a part of herself just to please him? What would she do if she couldn't act on this new fantasy of hers?

"So that's it then? No more Jay?" Mike said finally.

"I'm not sure honestly. This whole experience has been so...amazing. I don't want to stop exploring this but I don't want it to affect us in any way. I want to do it with someone who ends up like Jay who tries to manipulate me into being his alone. I'm looking for dick , not a new partner."

"I'm going to take that as a compliment," Mike said chuckling. "I guess I should be glad that you don't want to sacrifice us while you explore. Honestly it was one of my biggest fears when this whole thing started. What if that other guy steals her away from me, you know? But I feel better now having heard you explain how you feel."

"Of course, love. And I appreciate you being so understanding so far." Sam said, leaning over and giving her husband a small kiss on the cheek.

Mike smiled, cupping the part of his cheek that she had kissed. "You're welcome, you know I want you to feel free to explore. Anything that makes you happy."

"Yeah, but I don't know how to do that in a way that doesn't involve sacrifice."

Mike went into deep thought then set his mug down. "Maybe we need to find people like you."

"What do you mean?" Sam said, setting her own mug down.

"Maybe we're coming at this from the wrong angle. We've been looking for unattached men and that has the potential to get messy but maybe we need to get with people like us. It's less risky than going solo with random guys who can get possessive." Mike suggested.

"I'm not understanding, Mike."

"Look, I'm just saying there's got to be people like us out there. Maybe you can find a man who is like you and the both of you can do your thing."
Sam thought it over. "That's actually not a bad idea actually and it could be a way for us to keep things exciting. Would you be open to that?"

Mike wrapped his arms around her, pulling her close. "I'm open to it. How about this, let's just take it slow and figure this out together. No pressure. Let's go online and find out more then go from there?"
Sam nodded. "I like the sound of that."

CHAPTER TWO: The Invitation

Sam and Mike decided that the best place to start was online, so they spent the next few days doing research. On the hotwives forum where Sam posted her experiences when she started her journey, they posted what they were looking for and got a ton of suggestions from people who had been in that lifestyle for years.

"It sounds like you might be interested in swinging! Why don't you try this site? My husband and I found a couple that we are both so comfortable with and that we're all married makes us feel more secure about our connection."

"Swinging," Mike started, looking over Sam's shoulder at the computer in front of her, "that seems like a good start."

"What even is that?" Sam asked, looking at the computer with a confused expression on her face. "It feels like we're always coming across new terms all the time, it's hard to keep up."

Mike squinted at the computer screen then typed in the word 'swinging' in the search engine. "Says here it's when one or both partners engage in sexual activities with other people. Some people prefer to do it with other partnered people, oh like us! That's what we're looking for."

"I suppose that does sound like us." Sam said, feeling nerves coming on. This was all very overwhelming but there was an undercurrent of excitement in the midst of it all.

"There's a site where we can join, connect with other couples. Ready to give it a shot?" Mike asked, looking over at his wife.

Sam swallowed then nodded, no choice but to dive in.

The site was surprisingly enlightening for them. Not only was it a place to connect with other people, it also educated about the lifestyle with tips and cautionary tales to be mindful of. All over the site, it seemed to emphasize one thing; communication. Anyone who wanted to get involved in this had to keep their partner in the loop every step of the way.

"Communicate, that seems easy enough right?" Sam said, looking over to her husband.

Mike nodded. "I don't have anything to hide from you."

They registered themselves on the site, posting pictures of themselves, their interests and what they were into. After that, they added some information about themselves and logged off with the intention of signing back after a few days to check on their progress.

A couple of days later, they logged back in and went through the latest posts and some couples who had shown interest in their profiles. Just at that moment, a message popped up in their inbox from a couple named Andre and Leila.

"They seem friendly." Mike said, leaning closer to the screen. He read the message aloud as Sam wasn't with her glasses.

'Hi Sam and Mike, we noticed you're a little new to all of this so allow us to introduce ourselves. We're Andre and Leila, an interracial couple that lost meeting like-minded couples. We're hosting a private event this weekend and would love you to come through. It's a small gathering, just a few couples getting to know each other in an intimate environment. It might be the perfect introduction to this lifestyle. No pressure, just come through if you can. Looking forward to connecting!'

'This was it', Sam thought with excitement. This was the perfect way to get into the flow of things. "What do you think?"

"I think it sounds perfect. We can meet Andre and Leila as well as other couples like us. Let's do it."

The event was in two days and it came faster than the both of them expected. Before they knew it, they were driving up to the address that Andre and Leila had given them. It was a fancy neighborhood and that made Sam nervous and very aware of the fact that they were about to enter a space filled with complete strangers.

They pulled up to a sleek house at the end of a cul-de-sac and got out of the car. Sam took a deep breath, smoothing down her dress. She had spent a lot of time picking out her outfit - a body hugging black gown that made her feel really sexy but wasn't too revealing. She took her husband's hand and together, they walked up to the door of the house.

They knocked on the door and waited for a while before it was opened. The sound of the soft bass music hit them first before they took in the man that was in front of them. It was a tall, muscular man with high-top hair and a warm smile. He had dark skin and was wearing a tight white shirt that contrasted it. Sam recognized him immediately, he was Andre, the man who had invited her tonight.

"You must be Mike," he said, extending a handshake which Mike accepted. He turned to Sam and gave her a lingering, hungry look. "And you must be Sam, I'm glad you could make it out."

"Happy to be here and thank you for inviting us. I have to admit, I wasn't expecting such a handsome young man to be the host of this party." Sam said, taking a look inside to catch a glimpse of what was happening inside.

Andre laughed, a deep attractive sound. "Young? I haven't been young since I was in my thirties. But I appreciate the compliment. Please come in, let me introduce you to Leila and some of the people we know."

Sam and Mike stepped in, taking in the environment. They were led into a large living room where small groups of people were gathered with drinks in their hands. Some groups of people were making out, hands everywhere and in a little corner, an orgy was about to start.

Sam's eyes bulged. "I didn't know this was that kind of party."

"It's mostly a mixer but some people can't help themselves sometimes. You don't have to do anything you're not comfortable with but if you do feel like getting dirty, there's lube and condoms available. Now where's my wife, I want her to meet you two."

A petite woman approached them then wrapped her arms around Andre before giving him a small peck on his lips. "I've been looking everywhere for you, you left me alone to play host." The petite woman said, pulling away fro Andre and giving him a pouty face.

"I'm sorry, I had to get the door. Leila, I want you to meet Sam and Mike, they just arrived." Andre said, turning to face Sam and Mike.

"Oh yes, I recognize them! The cute couple from that site. I'm so glad you two could make it." Leila said, hugging Sam then Mike for a couple seconds too long.

Andre and Leila took them around the room, introducing them to other couples and placing some drinks in their hands. Mike and Sam started to relax and soon they were on a couch with Andre and Leila, slightly tipsy and heavily flirting.

Leila sat on Andre's thighs, her hands in his hair. Sam felt a little envy watching the two of them. They behaved like newly in love teenagers, handsy and jovial.

"If you don't mind me asking, how old are you two?" Sam said, blurting out the question before she could really think it through.

Andre and Leila looked at each other then burst into laughter. "I know we look a little young but please don't hold it against us." Andre said, his laughter settling into a light chuckle.

"I'm 45 years old and Leila here is 40."

Sam opened her eyes wide. "Wow, I wish I looked that good at 40."

Andre smirked and looked her over. "I don't know what you're talking about, you look really good right now. That dress is very...alluring." He said, his eyes lingering on her body.

Sam could feel heat creep onto her face and then she felt it start to creep downwards. Andre was a very attractive man, no doubt about that and he definitely had an effect on her.

The evening crept on and the atmosphere started to get a little more charged. The more people drank, the more loose they became and soon people began pairing off, leaning into each other and heavily making out. Andre and Leila didn't seem interested in what was happening around them, their eyes were completely focused on Sam and Mike.

Sam on the other hand was very interested in everything that was happening. She caught sight of a pair not too far from them, the woman was sitting in the man's lap and they were kissing deeply. Another couple was openly making out on the arm of the sofa near them.

"It's a lot, I know," Andre said, smiling slightly. "But it can be pretty fun."

"Do you guys always host sex parties?" Sam blurted out again, earning a laugh from Mike who was deep into his fifth beer.

Andre and Leila laughed again. "They weren't always sex parties, in a way they still aren't. We just saw a need for people to get together if they were interested in swinging or sharing partners and then we found that people also needed a safe space to do their thing. So we said, 'why not our place?'" Leila said.

"Do you ever get involved?" Mike asked.

"Only with people that we really like." Andre said, his voice dripping with innuendo. As he said that, Leila got off his thighs and sat beside Mike. Sam looked over at Andre and he beckoned her over. When she got closer to him, he made her sit on his lap in Leila's place then whispered in her ears, 'and we really like you.'

His hands crept up her thigh then under her dress. He leaned closer and kissed behind her ears, whispering softly in an alluring voice, "If I'm doing anything you're not comfortable with, let me know and I'll stop."

Sam swallowed as his hand continued creeping up her thigh whilst the other one cupped her neck. She turned her head and saw Mike and Leila watching them intently, clearly both aroused by what they were watching.

This was it, they were finally getting into the swing of things.

CHAPTER THREE: The Next Step

By now, Andre's hand had found what it was looking for, shifting Sam's panties and playing with her clit. Hr brought his mouth away from Sam's ear and to her neck, nibbling slightly then sucking while his hand worked its magic. Sam inhaled sharply as Andre moved his finger in circles over her clit and she could feel herself getting increasingly aroused.

Mike watched as yet another man claimed his wife in front of him. Under normal circumstances, this would be incredibly arousing and it still was but she could see Leila's eyes going over their partners before returning to him and he had no idea how to feel with her watching them.

The party was in full swing now, the alcohol and the dim lighting making for the perfect breeding ground for exploring. Most people around them had shed their clothes and were giving each other head whilst others were content with simply using their lips to explore as much of each other as they could without taking their clothes off.

Andre slipped the finger that had been working Sam's clit into her, causing her to let out a loud sigh. He turned her face towards him and crashed his lips against hers. His kiss was harsh and full of thinly veiled desire. Jay's kisses had been controlled but Andre's were wild, he had no intention of hiding how much he wanted Sam and it made her feel powerful, being this desired by other men.

Leila cleared her throat and Andre pulled away from Sam, his eyes darkened by desire. "Perhaps we should take this upstairs?" She proposed.

"Upstairs?" Mike asked, looking between Leila and Andre.

Andre smirked. "Of course. Or would you prefer I fuck your wife on the sofa you're sitting on?"

Mike blinked, the comment sending an instant shock of arousal through him. He turned to Leila, in an attempt to gauge how much of this she was okay with and she nodded. Andre made Sam stand before he got off the chair. He took Sam's hand and started leading her upstairs with Mike and Leila following behind them.

Sam turned around to see Mike and Leila following them. She looked at her husband and he gave her a subtle nod. They had talked about the possibility of something like this happening if they came for this party and now that it was becoming a reality, they were prepared for it. But Sam had to admit to herself that it was both thrilling and terrifying, this was only the second man she would be sleeping with since she started this whole journey and she couldn't help but wonder how she would measure up.

Her pulse quickened as they headed up the staircase. Andre turned towards her and gave her a reassuring smile which calmed her a little bit but not by much. The room he led them to was very spacious with the same soft lighting that was in the area they just left.

Andre closed the door behind them as Mike and Leila made their way into the room. He walked over to Sam and gently brushed a strand of hair behind her ear, his touch sending a thrill down her spine.

Mike sat on the armchair opposite the bed and Leila took a seat on the arm, both watching their partners intensely. Sam turned to look at them but Andre cupped her face and made her look at him.

"Forget about them. Forget that there is anyone else in this room and focus on me, only me." He leaned closer and buried his face in the crook of her neck, inhaling her scent. His hands came around her waist and grabbed her ass while he let out a soft growl.

"I can work with this." He said, squeezing her asscheeks then spanking them lightly. He brought his lips up to hers and kissed them softly, like he was testing the waters. Sam responded almost immediately, very turned on by the way Andre was taking control of the situation. He slipped his tongue into her mouth, exploring, tasting, familiarizing himself with the taste of her.

By this point, Andre was sporting a very pronounced erection. He walked Sam over to the nearby bed and pushed her into it, her breath coming out in soft gasps as Andre explored her with his hand. He grinded his erection against her, his hands moving to cup her breasts. He took his mouth away from her lips and brought them down to her chest, taking a nipple in his mouth and sucking it through her dress.

Sam threw her head back, sighing with content when she felt the wetness of his tongue as he swirled it around her nipple. She let out a gasp when he resumed sucking it with more intensity almost like a hungry child. As his mouth did its thing, one hand played with the other free nipple while the other slipped under her dress, shifting her panties to the side and penetrating her.

Andre was excited to find her already wet for him, he wanted nothing more than to skip all this preamble and bury himself inside her already but he knew he had to work her up, make her needy for him. He wanted her to beg for it before he had his way with her.

Mike could only watch as Andre fingered his wife on the bed in front of him and Leila. He was already sporting a boner and he wanted desperately to take it out of his pants and stroke it but he felt self conscious. This wasn't like the time with Jay, where it was just three of them. This time there was another pair of eyes, Leila's and he didn't know how he felt stroking himself in front of her.

But Leila wasn't the type of woman to just stand by and watch. She stood up and gingerly stepped in front of Mike, kneeling in front of him. Slowly, her hand felt up his boner and before Mike knew what was happening, she was unbuckling his pants and revealing his boner.

"What are you-" he couldn't finish his sentence because Leila's mouth quickly enveloped his dick before he could object. He let out a groan, a mix of pleasure and surprise as Leila's tongue circled and flicked against the head of his dick. She moaned as she bobbed her head up and down the shaft, earning soft gasps from Mike.

Sam heard the sounds Mike was making and turned her head, expecting to see him pleasuring himself. Instead she found Leila giving him what looked to be a very pleasurable blowjob and the red face of her husband absolutely enjoying it.

Andre took his mouth off her breast to check out what she was looking at then smirked before moving his finger faster within Sam. That brought her attention back to him as she started bucking her hips against his fingers, chasing the orgasm that was just on the horizon.

"I told you to focus on me," Andre snarled, before attacking her neck with his mouth, sucking at it hard enough to leave a mark. "Focus on how good this feels," he whispered against her neck as his finger moved faster within her. He used his thumb to circle her clit and the double stimulation was enough to send Sam over the edge.

Sam let out a long, strained moan as waves of pleasure came over her. Andre took the finger out of her then brought it up to his mouth, sucking her juices off them. She tasted sweet and Andre couldn't wait to know how she would feel when he was inside her.

Andre pushed himself off her then started unbuckling his pants, watching Sam intently as she sat up in bed, her face red and still clearly coming down from the orgasm she just experienced. "Take off your dress," he instructed, "slowly."

Sam made a show of stripping her dress of her body. She slowly raised the dress over her head, letting it drop to the floor before she unhooked her bra and took that off as well, before taking off her panties. Andre smiled as she cupped her breasts in her hands, making the look fuller.

"Fuck, I could do a lot with those. Fuck them, suck them, cum on them. There's so much I want to do to you, but for now, I need to fuck you." He said, letting his boxers drop to the floor, his huge dick standing at full attention.

He walked over to her with it in his hand, stoking it as he went along. When he stood in front of her, he traced the line of her lips with his head. "Do you see what she's doing?" He said, pointing over to Leila and Mike. Leila was holding Mike's dick in her hands and using her tongue to go up and down his shaft.

Sam nodded then looked back at Andre. "Think you can do that with this?" He pointed over to his dick that was leaking precum at this point. Sam gauged the penis in front of her face. She knew her way around a blowjob but she had never had a cock as big as Andre's in her mouth before.

"You don't have to-" Sam cut Andre off by taking his dick in her mouth, bobbing her head the way she saw Leila do earlier. "Fuck," Andre sighed, holding unto her head as his dick went in and out of Sam's mouth. The wetness and the heat of it sent shockwave after shockwave of pleasure up his body and he had to hold himself back from fucking the shit out of her mouth. Sam couldn't take the full length into her mouth but she took in what she could, tracing the head of his dick with her tongue and creating a vacuum of suction with her mouth.

She looked up at Andre and felt pride when she saw his eyes closed and his mouth open, clearly lost in the way she was sucking him. She felt the initial jealousy from watching Leila go down on Mike melt away, she could do that and even more with Andre.

Andre pushed her off him and she fell back onto the bed. He moved quickly, climbing on top of her then taking her lips harshly as he used his dick head to stroke her clit.

"I want to be inside you so bad." he groaned as he positioned himself at her entrance. He slid into her slowly, trying to get her used to the fullness of him. Sam gasped and held on to him as he buried himself fully into her.

Mike looked on as Andre thrusted into his wife, moaning as he did so. He took pride in the way Andre's mouth fell open as he moved in her, his thrusts getting more and more intense. Watching that sight and feeling the way Leila was stroking him was enough to make him burst and he came loudly, pouring cum into Leila's mouth which she happily received.

Whilst Leila cleaned up the mess that Mike had made with her mouth, Andre was driving himself into Sam forcefully. She took him eagerly, even raising her hips to meet every thrust he gave her. Andre took pleasure in the way she wrapped her legs around him, making him go deeper into her and he let out all the pent up desire he had felt earlier.

"Fuckkk," He said, leaning over and pounding into her repeatedly. She was so wet and the sound of him penetrating her was driving him over the edge. "I'm going to cum," he groaned, giving three more intense thrusts before pulling himself out of Sam and cumming all over her stomach.

"Shit," he said, chuckling as he caught his breath. "we're going to have to do this again soon."

CHAPTER FOUR:
Dangerous Dealings

It had been a couple of days since the very intense night at Andre and Leila's house and even though Sam and Mike discussed briefly, they both tried to avoid talking about it as much as they could. The dynamic was very new — this was the first time that Mike had been involved with someone during one of their encounters and they both didn't know what to make of it.

Sam often replayed the parts of the night where she watched Leila go down on her husband, even though it was an exciting sight she couldn't help but feel a little jealousy whenever she thought about it. Despite these feelings, she and Mike accepted an invitation from Andre and Leila to lunch at a diner central to the four of them.

The drive to the diner was quiet. Mike seemed to be preoccupied, his gaze fixed on the road but still oddly distracted. Sam opened her mouth to ask what was on his mind when his phone buzzed in the cup holder. He glanced at the screen then declined the call only for it to buzz again as the same person called again.

Sam noticed the furrow in his brow as he declined the call again and put the phone down. "Who was that?" she asked, trying to keep her tone casual even though she was a little suspicious.

"Just work stuff," Mike said with a dismissive shrug.

"Work stuff on a Saturday?" Sam asked, finding that a little suspicious. "Is everything okay?"

"It's fine, Sam. Drop it." Mike said quickly, too quickly. "There's nothing to worry about, I'll reach out to them later. Let's just focus on lunch, okay?"

Sam decided not to push further, but she couldn't help but feel a little suspicious and uneasy. She brushed off the feeling though, deciding to focus on the lunch that was supposed to be an opportunity to get to know Andre and Leila better. The last thing she wanted was to bring any tension between her and Mike into it.

When they got to the diner, they found Andre and Leila already there, sitting in a booth with some drinks in front of them. Leila welcomed them with a bright smile and Andre gave Sam a lingering look before standing up to hug her and shake Mike's hand.

"We're so glad the both of you could make it." Leila said, settling into the booth beside Mike.

"We're happy we could make it. Have you guys put in an order yet?" Sam asked.

"No, not yet, we've only gotten a few drinks. We were actually waiting for you two to show up before we had anything." Andre said, handing a menu over to Sam. "Anything look good?"

Sam looked over the menu then shook her head. "I'm not really hungry, I think I'll just have a couple of iced teas." She said. Andre signaled to the waitress who took Sam's drink order. Turning to Mike, he asked him if he was interested in anything but Mike didn't answer, seemingly engrossed by his phone.

"Mike? Man, you want anything while the waitress's here?" Andre pressed but Mike didn't answer. Leila nudged Mike and he looked up to find the entire booth looking at him and the waitress waiting patiently to take his drink order. He shook his head no, saying he wasn't interested in anything then went back to his phone.

"Mike's been dealing with some work today, I haven't even had a bit of his attention today." Sam said in a joking tone, trying to take away from the awkwardness Mike's focus on his phone was bringing.

Andre chuckled then wrapped an arm around Sam before whispering in her ear, "I guess I have to show you twice as much attention today." His statement sent goosebumps down her body. At that moment, her iced tea order came over and she eagerly downed it to calm herself down before ordering for another.

"So how long have you guys been swingers?" Sam asked, taking a sip from her iced tea then dropping it on the table.

Leila and Andre looked at each other before Leila smiled and answered. "I think the both of us have always had a healthy curiosity about things like that. We both had open relationships when we were single and this is just a natural progression of that."

"We've been in it for over five years now?" Andre asked, looking over to his wife for confirmation who then nodded. "So yeah, five years. We decided to keep our encounters with just couples because it was less messy."

Leila nodded. "The last unattached person we got involved with tried to come in between Andre and me so we both decided we don't want that type of energy in our marriage."

Sam perked up as she took a sip from her drink. "That's exactly what happened to Mike and me! Wow, what a coincidence."

"We knew you two would understand, that's why we decided to reach out. Even though we've been in this for sometime now, it's still hard to find like-minded couples." Leila said.

Sam nodded before finishing off her third glass of iced tea. "Oof, these drinks went right through me. Excuse me for a moment." She said, getting up and heading for the nearest bathroom.

She finished up and walked towards the sink, washing her hands then splashing some water on her face. She took a deep breath before turning to head back to the booth when the bathroom door creaked open. Andre slipped in, then approached her, a sly grin on his face,

"What are you doing here?" Sam whispered, her pulse quickening.

"I couldn't resist." Andre said, stepping closer to her till he was just inches away from her face. "You've been on my mind all week and I just couldn't wait."

Her breath hitched when Andre's hand found her waist and pulled her against him. "Someone might be in here." she whispered urgently.

"Then they're in for quite the show." He whispered before claiming her lips. Andre's hand wrapped around her back before slipping into her blouse and cupping her right breast. He took his mouth to her neck and kissed it, before sucking on it again.

"I really fucking want you right now," he said, breathing onto her neck. He pulled away then inspected her neck. "Looks like I left a mark last time, is it wrong that I want to leave another one?"

Sam shook her head and Andre returned his mouth to her neck, sucking at it hungrily. Her hands reached for the front of his pants and sure enough, she could feel a bulge forming. She looked around then quickly pulled him into a nearby stall.

When the both of them were safely obscured by the stall, Andre worked on taking her top off then slipped two fingers between her legs and into her. A gasp left Sam's lips causing Andre to smirk.

"You're already so wet, I love that about you." He said before tracing circles on her clit with his thumb while his two fingers moved within her. He freed a nipple from her bra and sucked on it, following Sam's senses with pleasure. She bit his shirley to cover her moans but Andre wasn't having any of that.

"I want to hear every single sound you make," he said, his fingers moving faster within her.

"But what if someone hears us?" Sam asked, still trying to keep her voice low.

"I really don't give a fuck." he said, increasing the intensity of the strokes his fingers were making inside of her. Sam threw her head back in reckless abandon and let her moans come out without any inhibition.

"Yes, that's it." Andre said, "Let it all out."

Sam buckled slightly as she came all over his fingers. He took his fingers out of her then brought them to her lips, imploring her to suck on them. "I want you to know how you taste and understand why it's so hard to resist you."

Sam sucked herself off his fingers and when she was done with that, he turned her around and bent her over, hurriedly taking his dick out and coating it with the juices between her legs.

He pushed himself into her, sighing as he did so. He presses her into the wall with each of his hard thrusts, the sound of his thighs slapping against her ass filling the air.

His hands came around and grabbed her tits while he drove himself into her. Sam could fill another orgasm building up and she backed herself up against him, begging him to go faster. Andre pounded into her faster and harder, feeling himself getting closer each time he buried himself in her.

Sam felt herself cum one more time and that seemed to be enough to drive Andre over the edge. His breath started to quicken and he moved in her faster. He leaned closer and sighed into her ear, "Fuck, this feels too fucking good."

He grunts, thrusting in one more time before pulling out of her and cumming all over the bathroom floor.

Meanwhile, back at the booth, Mike could barely focus on what Leila was saying because his phone kept buzzy and he knew that he couldn't keep ignoring it.

"That phone keeps buzzing her, you can take it, I don't mind." Leila said.

"Yeah I'm sorry, just give me a moment, I need to take this." Mike muttered, sliding out of the booth and stepping out of the diner. Now that he was alone, he could answer the call.

"You've been dodging my calls, Mike. You know the clock's ticking on this shipment, it needs to leave tonight or do I have to give this job to someone more reliable?" A gruff voice said on the other end of the phone.

Mike's jaw clenched. "We're still on for this deal. I'll get the shipment out before the day is over, just give me a bit more time."

"*Fine, just get this done quickly.*" The gruff voice said again before ending the call.

Mike shoved his phone back into his pocket, trying to settle his anxiety over the call he just had. When he returned to the booth, he forced a smile for Leila, trying to keep himself together.

Back in the bathroom, Sam and Andre straightened themselves out and headed out, Sam first and then Andre. When they rejoined Mike and Leila back at the booth, Sam could notice a tension in Mike even though he tried to hide it. She decided not to mention it till they got home.

CHAPTER FIVE: The Confrontation

Sam was awake in bed, staring at the ceiling as the clock ticked midnight. This was the third time this week that Mike had told her that he was working late and now he wasn't even back home. Normally she would brush it off, this wasn't the first time in their marriage that he had to stay out late for work but something about this was different. He was more guarded lately, more distant and distracted and she couldn't help but feel a little suspicious.

What could he possibly be doing? When he went out like this he was always vague. "I'm staying out late for work." he would say but what was he doing exactly? If something happened to him, what would she even tell the authorities, that she didn't know what her husband was up to at midnight?

She thought back to that night where he had hooked up with Leila. Was he cheating maybe? Sam hated that her mind went in that direction but she couldn't help it, without context her mind had to fill in the gaps however it decided it wanted to.

She knew she wasn't exactly innocent either. With Mike spending time outside so much, she had spent a lot more time with Andre than she had wanted to. He made her feel desired and wanted whereas her husband seemed to be avoiding her. She couldn't help herself but to seek Andre out.

The sound of the front door creaking open snapped her out of her late night thoughts and she sat up, listening as Mike's footsteps got closer and closer. She heard the clear sound of him fumbling with his keys, trying but failing to be quiet.

He walked into their bedroom and she flicked the lamp on, the sudden light making him squint and catching him off guard. "You're still up?" he asked, trying his best to sound casual as he took his shoes off.

"I couldn't sleep," she mumbled. "Where were you?"

"I told you before I left Sam, work stuff." You know I have to pull long hours sometimes."

"I don't know what it is you're doing that keeps you out till midnight? Do you have any idea how scary it is thinking you're out on the road in that truck, doing God knows what? What if something happened to you?"

Mike let out a frustrated sigh, this was not what he wanted to come back to after the day he had.

"Look, I don't think I need to justify myself to you, not now. You know how demanding my job can be."

"Oh I do, especially nowadays." She shot back. "Things are different now though, you're always distracted like the time at the diner and I can't help but wonder what's really going on."

Mike froze for a moment, not expecting his wife to call him out like that. Guilt flickered across his face for a brief moment but he quickly masked it with a dismissive shake of his head. "You're overthinking this, Sam."

"Am I?" Sam said, her voice rising. "This wouldn't have anything to do with this lifestyle would it? I know things are moving pretty fast but that doesn't mean that you have to hide things from me, I'm your wife."

Mike tightened his jaw as he looked at her. "You really want to get into this Sam? Fine, let's get into it. Let's not pretend that you haven't been getting real cozy with Andre behind my back?"

"I have no idea what you mean."

"Oh please, don't play dumb. At the diner that day, I know what you two got up to and I know you've been getting it this week when I've been out of the house. So don't come at me, talking about secrets when you've been keeping yours from me." Mike said, frustration bleeding into his voice.

"Don't make this out into a bigger deal than it is. We both agreed on Andre and Leila. You were there when we first hooked up, in fact you did the same thing with Leila."

"Yeah but the difference is, anything I did was not behind your back. You were right there when I did whatever I did with Leila but have you told me or even brought me into any of the trysts you've had with Andre recently?"

Sam kept quiet, guilt spreading on her face. "Okay I know that I haven't been completely honest but that doesn't explain the late night or all the calls you keep dodging when you're around me."

"Let it go Sam, geez. I am exhausted, I need to go to bed and you are making me so stressed out." Mike said. He knew that he couldn't keep dodging her forever but he couldn't lay it all out there for her, not now.

"Look Sam, this is business okay? And I'm handling it. So can't we just let it go and go to bed?"

"Fine," she said, her voice weary. "But don't think this is over, Mike." She turned away from Mike, pulling the covers up as she felt all the exhaustion hit her all at once. This confrontation had drained her emotionally and she didn't feel like arguing anymore. Just as she was settling into bed, her phone buzzed on her nightstand. She picked up, looking at the notification on her screen.

It was a message from Andre.

Her heart skipped a beat as she read the text: "*Thinking about you. Can we meet tomorrow? I miss our time together.*"

Before she could even process the message that came in, she felt Mike's presence behind her, his eyes narrowing as he leaned over to see the screen.

"Seriously, Sam?" His voice was cold, the frustration from earlier creeping back in. "You're seriously planning another meetup right in front of me?"

Sam tensed, already knowing where this was headed. "It's not like that! I haven't even responded. "

"Oh but you were going to, what were you going to do? Sneak off to see him while I'm busting my ass off out there? " Mike scoffed, crossing his arms.

"Oh c'mon. You just said you were exhausted and now you're bringing up another argument out of nowhere? " Sam shot back,

"Don't play the victim here!" Mike's voice rose, his anger clear. "We agreed that if we're going to do this, it would be with communication and transparency. But you're keeping secrets now, seeing Andre without telling me. That was never part of the deal, Sam."

"Maybe I wouldn't be doing it if you weren't so focused on whatever shady business you're mixed up in," Sam snapped. "Disappearing late at night, taking calls you won't explain? You're shutting me out, Mike, so can you really blame me for looking for a way to keep busy? —

"You're not the only one with issues, Sam." Mike said, his expression now shifting to one of hurt. "I've been dealing with the fact that you're getting closer to Andre, more than we agreed to. I see how you look at him, how you're letting this become more than just sex. And what about me, Sam? I don't mind what you do with him but why are you hiding it from me?"

Sam felt her defenses falter, guilt gnawing at her. "Yeah well, now you know how I felt watching Leila feel you up that night." She said, in an effort to mask her guilt.

"That was different and you know it. You were there, you didn't say anything afterward, I thought you were okay with it."

"Well I wasn't. It was hot yeah but it wasn't part of the deal either, I was blindsided and the most annoying part is, we never even talked about it afterward."

Mike's jaw tightened, his voice low. "So what do we do now, Sam? The whole point of doing this was so things wouldn't get messy but it looks like it's too late for that."

"I don't know. But I do know that this isn't what I wanted. I thought exploring this would bring us closer, that it would be something we could share together. But now...I don't want to fight about this anymore."

Mike sighed. "You're right. I don't want to fight either. We stopped being honest with each other, and now we're both doing things we said we wouldn't."

A heavy silence hung between them as they both struggled to find the right words. Finally, Sam took a deep breath, her voice softer now. "Maybe we need to stop seeing Andre and Leila. It's clear this isn't working for either of us. We've lost sight of what really matters—us."

Mike nodded slowly, though the decision felt bittersweet. "Yeah. This was supposed to be the solution to our problem but now it feels like it's coming between us, just like Jay tried to." ,

"Maybe we need to take a step back and figure out how to come back at this?"

"I think that's a good idea. So that's it, no more Andre and Leila?"

Sam nodded, although she felt that was a decision that was hard to make. She would miss Andre but nothing was worth losing the trust her husband had in her.

CHAPTER SIX: The Proposal

Mike stopped doing late-night deliveries for a couple of days. Anytime the dealer called him, he would make up an excuse on why he couldn't go. He did this to prevent any more fights between him and Sam. They had promised to be more honest so this was his way of doing that. Things seemed to be going okay, that is until they got an invitation from Andre and Leila.

They hadn't heard from them since Sam ignored the text Andre sent. Now he reached out again, sending an invitation to another swinger's party, with the promise of new faces and opportunities to meet others in the lifestyle.

"What do you think about this?" Sam asked Mike, showing him the message that evening while they were having dinner. "I know what we said," she began carefully, watching his reaction. "But don't you think this would be a good opportunity?"

"A good opportunity to do what?" Mike asked, chewing his food a little bit too loudly.

"To meet other people. We don't have to get involved with Andre and Leila but that doesn't mean we have to give up this lifestyle, you like it right?"

Mike thought about it and she was right, he did enjoy these sexcapades of theirs and he had to admit that it felt a little hard giving all of that up so easily. "You're right, I do like it,"

"So what do you say? We can go as a couple and just have fun then see what's out there."

"So we go to the party for us, not for them?"

"Exactly." Sam nodded. "No strings, no pressure. We can keep to ourselves if we want. We've talked about how we might be interested in exploring this lifestyle with other people, right? This could be a good way to dip our toes in without getting too deep too fast."

Mike was quiet for a moment, his gaze fixed on the invite on Sam's phone. Part of him was wary, it hadn't been long since they'd agreed to distance themselves from Andre and Leila, and going back into that environment felt like a risk. But on the other hand, he didn't want to retreat into the comfort of the routine their sex life had become prior to these new adventures Sam got involved in.

"I'm in but no secrets this time okay?"

"Deal." Sam's smile widened, relieved that they were on the same page. "This could be fun, you know? We're finally figuring out how to do this in a way that works for us."

"So when's the party?" Mike asked, going back to his food.

"It's tomorrow. Gosh, I wonder what I'm going to wear."

"Just wear any old dress, you'll look gorgeous." Mike responded.

The next day came by pretty quickly and soon Mike and Sam were on their way to the party. The party was already in full swing by the time they showed up. It was pretty similar to the first one, taking place in Andre and Leila's big suburban house, filled to the brim with people that were dressed to impress.

But this time, the action started earlier than expected. As they made their way through the main room, they couldn't help but notice couples already indulging openly in one another, the air thick with the scent of sex and alcohol.

Sam tried to ignore the growing heat in her body as they passed groups lounging on velvet couches, hands and lips exploring freely. Mike walked beside her, his hand resting possessively on the small of her back. They passed by a couple who were having sex on a nearby couch and headed deeper into the house, in search of Andre and Leila.

The sound of laughter drew their attention toward the bar where they spotted Andre and Leila, effortlessly mingling with the other guests. Sam's heart skipped a beat when she laid eyes on Andre. She hadn't been sure what it would feel like seeing them again but there was no doubt about it, this couple was still as charismatic as ever.

As if sensing their presence, Andre turned and locked eyes with them, his smile widening. He nudged Leila, and the couple made their way over, greeting Sam and Mike with warmth.

"I'm so glad you two could make it," Andre said, his deep voice smooth as ever. He leaned in to kiss Sam's cheek, lingering just a moment longer than polite. Leila greeted Mike the same way, a knowing glint in her eyes as she pulled back.

"We wouldn't miss it," Sam replied, trying to keep her voice steady despite the nerves tingling under her skin. Mike nodded, gripping his wife's hand a little tighter.

Leila waved over a server holding a tray of colorful cocktails. "You have to try these, they're a house specialty," she said, handing them each a glass. "They'll help you loosen up."

Sam eyed the drink cautiously before taking a sip. It was strong, much stronger than she expected, but the flavors masked the potency. Mike took a long swallow and raised his eyebrows in surprise. "They weren't kidding," he muttered under his breath, making Sam chuckle.

With drinks in hand, Leila and Andre led them to a waiter corner where the music wasn't loud. They exchanged some small talk, sipping the drinks in their hands. Sam could feel herself getting more comfortable and she eyed the couples she could see in the soft lighting, wondering which one of them would make a good new conquest.

Andre noticed her wandering eyes and then cleared his throat. "Listen guys, we have to confess that we had an ulterior motive inviting you out here tonight."

"Oh?" Sam said, the buzz from the cocktails making her mind fuzzy.

Andre looked at his wife and she nodded. "We've been thinking," he said, his gaze shifting between Sam and Mike. "We had such a good time together, and we think there's more potential here... something a bit more long-term, if you're open to it."

Leila chimed in, her voice excited. "We're talking about something exclusive, a regular arrangement between just the four of us. No need to search for new partners every time. We're all comfortable with each other, so why not take this to the next level? Andre likes being with you Sam and I like being with Mike so we could make this a regular partner swap till whenever we decide to end it."

Sam wasn't sure how she felt about this, she looked over at Mike but it was like his mind wasn't even here. He was unusually quiet and he had been glancing at his phone more than once, fidgeting like he was anxious.

Andre took Sam to a corner and leaned closer to her "So, what do you think?" he asked smoothly, "A long-term arrangement between just us four makes sense, doesn't it? We've already established trust, and it's clear we have chemistry."

Sam bit her lip. She was about to respond when she noticed movement out of the corner of her eye. Mike was excusing himself from Leila, his expression tight as he muttered something and walked away with his phone clutched in his hand.

"I'll be right back," Sam said to Andre, forcing a smile as she moved to follow Mike. Andre's eyes followed her, wondering what this was about.

Sam trailed Mike down a dim hallway that led away from the main area of the party. She could hear his voice as she approached, the tension in his tone unmistakable.

"I said I'm handling it," Mike hissed into the phone, his back turned to her. "I don't need you threatening me, I'll have the shipment moved tonight. Just back off, or we're done." His voice dropped lower, but the edge in it was clear. "You think sending me those texts was smart? I don't care who you are; you push me, and I'll push back harder."

Sam's heart lurched at his words. Shipment? Threats? Her mind raced with questions, trying to piece together what she was overhearing.

She stepped closer, her pulse pounding. "Mike, what the hell is going on?" she demanded.

Mike spun around, startled. For a split second, guilt flashed across his face before it hardened into a defensive expression. "It's nothing, Sam," he said quickly, slipping his phone into his pocket. "Just work stuff. You wouldn't understand."

"Work stuff, again?" Sam scoffed, crossing her arms. "You're talking about shipments at a party? You've been acting weird all night, what is going on?"

Mike's eyes darted around as if searching for the right words. He opened his mouth to speak, but Sam cut him off, her voice rising. "What are you really involved in, Mike? What have you been hiding?"

Before he could answer, the sound of approaching footsteps interrupted them. Andre appeared, a concerned look on his face. "Everything okay here?" he asked, glancing between them with a raised eyebrow.

Sam shot Andre a sharp look. "Not really. But I'm handling it, please give me a second."

Andre nodded and walked away, leaving Sam and Mike alone.

Mike's jaw clenched, the tension in his body palpable. He was cornered, and he knew it.

"Well Mike? I'm waiting, what's the excuse this time?"

What was Mike hiding exactly?

THE END

Dear reader,

Thank you for reading to the end! I hope the book lived up to your expectations!

Would you like to read part three? It's available at Amazon as well; just go to this book's product page or series page!

Exclusive erotic short story club

Want even more? You can join my exclusive erotic short club **for free**. By doing so, you will get a bunch of free stories (before I publish them on Amazon), audiobook coupon codes, and much more! Join here:

https://bit.ly/3WJsqRp

Or email me at amber.carden.books@gmail.com and I will send you a link!

Amber

© Copyright 2024 - All rights reserved.

The content contained within this book may not be reproduced, duplicated, or transmitted without direct written permission from the author or the publisher.

This book is copyright protected. It is only for personal use. You cannot amend, distribute, sell, use, quote or paraphrase any part, or the content within this book, without the consent of the author or publisher.

www.ingramcontent.com/pod-product-compliance
Lightning Source LLC
LaVergne TN
LVHW041629070526
838199LV00052B/3295